SECRET
OF OAK PARK

FICTION BY
KAREN GLENN
AND DENISE RINALDO

SCHOLASTIC INC.
New York   Toronto   London   Auckland   Sydney
Mexico City   New Delhi   Hong Kong

COVER ILLUSTRATION BY
JEFFREY LINDBERG

INTERIOR ILLUSTRATIONS BY
JODY JOBE

"Secrets of Oak Park" was first published as a 16-part serial in
Scholastic SCOPE® magazine, Vol. 44, 1995-1996.

Text copyright © 1995, 1996 by Scholastic Inc.
Illustrations copyright © 1999 by Scholastic Inc.
All rights reserved. Published by Scholastic Inc.
Printed in the U.S.A.

ISBN 0-439-05682-9

5 6 7 8 9 10   23   06 05 04

Table of Contents

Racist incidents turn Oak Park High School—and Kelly Rivera's life—upside down.

THE BEGINNING

Kelly Rivera squirmed in her seat. It was 9:30 on the first day of her junior year. She was supposed to be in the gym leading the Oak Park High cheerleading squad in its first practice of the season. Instead, she was sitting next to her best friend, Meredith Hall, in the hot, crowded auditorium. Kelly pushed her long, dark hair away from her face as they waited for the assembly to begin. She didn't know why Ms. Bauer, the school's new principal, had called the special meeting. All anyone knew was that the principal thought it was important enough to call them all out of class—or cheerleading practice.

Kelly thought back to the spring before. She'd been so excited when she'd been chosen captain of the cheerleading squad for the upcoming year. It had been the first time in school history that the job hadn't gone to a senior. That had definitely made people angry, Kelly remembered. For a while, it was the only thing that anyone wanted to talk about—until the incidents.

Kelly shuddered. She figured that the assembly probably had something to do with what had come to be called "the incidents," the horrible series of events that had hit the school—and the town—the spring before. It had all started with the racist graffiti spray painted in huge letters on the school's entryway. "Oak Park is for white people. Everyone else better watch out." Days later, the windows of stores in town owned by African Americans and Asians were smashed. The school, which was racially mixed, blew apart into fragments. White kids huddled together with white kids, black kids with black kids.

A voice from behind Kelly interrupted her thoughts. "Hey, wake up, Kelly! I've been looking all over for you!" Kelly turned to see Kai-Chu Wong, her boyfriend and the star forward on Oak Park's basketball team. Trim and muscular, he looked great in his new blue letter sweater. "I just heard that the cheerleaders . . ."

Before Kai could finish his sentence, a tall, imposing woman wearing bright red glasses walked on-stage. The room quickly fell silent as she tapped on the microphone. "I'm the new principal, Ms. Bauer," she began.

"Well, you'll see," Kai whispered. Kelly sat back nervously to listen.

"As you know, a series of unpleasant racial incidents have plagued our school and town. They have to stop, but they won't stop by themselves. To change things, we're all going to have to take action—and make sacrifices," Ms. Bauer said. "Let me tell you what's going to happen. First, every student will be required to attend a weekend retreat on diversity and tolerance." The students groaned.

Ms. Bauer ignored the moans and kept right on talking. "We're going to institute a school newspaper. That way, students will have a forum for speaking to and about each other in a civilized manner." The audience snickered, but Ms. Bauer didn't let their reaction stop her.

"Now comes the hard part. To pay for these programs and others you will hear about this week, we are making some cuts. We will eliminate these programs: lacrosse, one of the three school plays, the entire cheerleading squad. . . ."

Furious and in shock, Kelly didn't even hear the rest. Her friends reached out to comfort her, but she shrugged them away. Ms. Bauer finished her speech over jeers from the students. "Anyone interested in learning more about the newspaper should report to Room 23. Everyone else, go immediately to your scheduled classes."

"I have never been so angry in my entire life," Kelly whispered to Kai and Meredith as they left the auditorium. Her brown eyes shone with determination. "I'm going to that meeting. I'm going to tell them exactly how they've ruined my life."

"Meredith and I will go with you," said Kai. "Somebody has to stand up to them."

Kelly barged through the mass of students. Kai and

Meredith followed her. Room 23 was set up with chairs for fifty people, but almost all of them were empty. As Kelly sat down, she recognized the teacher in charge, Mr. Andropov. Short and round, he was known for his great memory—and his enormous mustache. She'd had him for freshman English.

The only other students in the room were two boys she didn't really know, but had seen around school. Hakim Moore, a good-looking African-American kid, never went anywhere without his camera. Zachary Springer, the ultimate nobody, walked around with a calculator sticking out of his pocket.

"Well, there are five students here, and we need only four for a newspaper staff," Mr. Andropov said, walking to the front of the room. "I'd say we're in pretty good shape."

"Hold on," Kelly broke in. "We're not here for the newspaper. We're here to protest."

"You're in luck. A newspaper is the best way in the world to protest," Mr. Andropov said, his enthusiasm making Kelly even angrier. "Let's get to work. Hakim, I know you're a photographer. We'll make you the photo editor."

"Okay," Hakim shrugged. He was trying to act like he didn't care, but Kelly could see he was excited.

"Zachary, you're a statistics whiz," Mr. Andropov said. "We'll put you in the sports editor slot."

Zach didn't bother trying to hide his happiness.

"Meredith, I know you hate English," Mr. Andropov said smiling. "We'll make you the business manager of the newspaper."

"She doesn't want to work on your newspaper, okay?" Kelly snapped.

"Meredith can speak for herself," Mr. Andropov replied. "Meredith, what do you say?"

Meredith nervously ran her hands through her wispy, blond hair. "I'll try," she said finally, her green eyes staring down at the floor. "I guess it could be interesting enough."

Kelly glared at her friend. Meredith was usually too shy to even introduce herself. What had come over her?

Mr. Andropov went on. "Kai, you're off the hook because you're committed to basketball. You won't have the time to devote to this. However, since there's no longer a cheerleading squad, Kelly will have lots of time and not much to do with it."

Kelly opened her mouth to say just what she thought of that remark. Before she could get a word out, Mr. Andropov interrupted.

"Kelly, you're the new editor-in-chief. I won't take no for an answer."

Meredith gets an anonymous tip, and things really start to heat up.

THE WAREHOUSE 2

A few weeks later, Kelly clutched the steering wheel of her mother's ancient red Volkswagon. She leaned forward, trying to see the traffic ahead of her through the blurry windshield. It had been drizzling when she'd pulled out of her driveway with Meredith and Hakim. Now it was pouring.

"Kelly, watch it!" Meredith cried from the back seat. Kelly swerved, narrowly missing a car that had pulled over to the side of the road to wait for the rain to stop.

"That guy seems to have the right idea," Hakim said. "Let's stop and wait till this storm is over."

Kelly shook her head. "No, I have to get my mom's car back in two hours so she can go to work. That means we have to check out that warehouse now. It could be a huge story for the paper."

At first, Kelly had refused to take the job of editor of the *Oak Park Beat*. Instead, she tried everything she could think of to get the school to reinstate the cheerleading squad. It was no use. She couldn't budge the school's tough new principal, Ms. Bauer.

"If you and your staff get to the bottom of the

incidents and help bring some harmony back to this school," Ms. Bauer had said, "we'll think about a cheerleading squad for the second semester."

As much as Kelly disliked Ms. Bauer, she was impressed that the principal thought that kids might be able to figure out who was behind the incidents. After all, adults—including the police, school officials, and a special task force—had failed. So Kelly decided to go ahead and work on the paper.

Back in Kelly's car, the rain on the windshield slowed a bit. Hakim started putting film in his camera.

"Now tell me all about this letter you got, Meredith," he said.

. "It was inside my locker when I got to school yesterday morning," Meredith said. "It wasn't signed or anything."

"I don't know if it's a real clue, or if somebody is just playing a big joke on us," Kelly added.

"It said—and I quote—'If you want to solve the incidents, you have to understand the motivation. Your quest should begin Saturday afternoon in the old Chambers Warehouse on Route 48.'"

Hakim rolled his eyes. "That's it? It's got to be a joke. Some morons somewhere are laughing like hyenas because we're running all over town for nothing. I'm sure of it."

"Maybe, maybe not," Kelly said, a little offended. She pulled the car to the side of the road. "Anyway, here we are."

The boarded-up building had once stored supplies for a furniture factory that had since closed down. Today it was empty. It was waiting to be torn down to make way for a new housing development. In the rainy gloom, it looked almost spooky.

"Well, let's go!" Kelly said in her best cheerleader voice. She hopped out of the car.

Hakim and Meredith glanced at each other. "She's crazy," Hakim whispered.

"A week ago she wouldn't even say the word 'newspaper.' Today she's Lois Lane."

The three silently walked up the long driveway to the warehouse. At the entrance, they noticed that a lock had been torn off the front door.

They stood there, not knowing what to do. Finally, Kelly spoke in a whisper. "Hakim, take your camera and come in with me. Meredith, stay out here. If we're not back in ten minutes, go get somebody. Take the car keys."

"I can't drive a stick," Meredith said, taking the keys, "but . . ." Before she could finish, Kelly and Hakim were gone.

Meredith looked at her watch. It was 2:35. She felt a little sick to her stomach. The rain was cold, and her umbrella had a little hole in it. She was feeling a little sorry for herself when she heard footsteps running inside the warehouse. Then they stopped. A second later, Meredith heard Kelly's terrified scream.

"It's a body! Oh, no! Meredith, do something!"

Kelly and Hakim find a body in the old Chambers warehouse—a very strange body.

THE BODY 3

Paralyzed with fear, Kelly and Hakim stared down at the pale, motionless form. Curled up in a corner of the warehouse entryway, the body looked peaceful—almost alive.

"It looks like he was a kid our age," Hakim whispered to Kelly.

Kelly took a deep breath. Then she whispered back, her voice shaky. "What could have happened to him? I don't even want to think about it. Let's try to be brave—for him. First go ahead and take a picture. Then let's get out of here."

Hakim raised his camera and took a photo. At that moment, in the glare of the flash, he realized whose body it was. He felt sick.

"It's Zach," Hakim said slowly. He was horrified, "Look! He's got that curly red hair. He's got freckles. It's Zach Springer!"

As Hakim spoke, Zach's body seemed to shudder and stretch out. Hakim and Kelly clutched each other and leaped backwards, both screaming.

"Hey, what are you guys yelling about?" Zach asked,

rubbing his eyes and standing up. "You're scaring me to death!"

"You're alive!" Kelly gasped.

"Of course I'm alive. Why wouldn't I be?"

Hakim crossed his arms and shook his head. "Springer, you're a true idiot. Meredith is probably calling the cops right now."

Just then, Meredith came rushing in. "I can't call the police!" she said breathlessly. "There's no telephone anywhere!"

"Calm down. The emergency is over," Hakim said, looking disgusted.

"I, um, fell asleep," Zach said.

"I knew this whole thing had to be a joke," Hakim said. "What exactly were you trying to prove, Springer? You were the one who left the note in Meredith's locker," he demanded, "weren't you?"

"I did leave the note, but it wasn't a joke. I just fell asleep waiting for you. It's not my fault that you thought I was dead."

"Listen, Zach," Kelly said kindly. "If you had something you wanted to show us, why didn't you just talk to us at school? You could have mentioned it in the newspaper office."

"To be honest, I was kind of scared," Zach said. "I know you all think I'm a loser. You probably wouldn't have listened to anything I had to say."

"Oh, stop whining and tell us what's going on," Hakim said. "You've got us where you want us."

Kelly sat down on an old barrel that had been left in the warehouse. Zach remained standing as the others made themselves comfortable on the dusty floor. The only light in the windowless room came through the open front door.

"I think some people my dad knows might have something to do with the racial incidents," Zach said, pacing nervously back and forth. "About a week ago, my mom was away on business and I was up in my room," Zach continued. "Nobody knows it, but from one corner of my room, I can hear everything that happens in the living room. My dad had some people down there, and they were laughing. I listened in. They were laughing about the incidents."

"They were laughing?" Kelly asked, shocked.

"Who were these guys?" Hakim asked.

"I don't know who they were," Zach answered. "I didn't go downstairs because I didn't want them to see me. I guess they were real estate guys like my dad."

"That still doesn't explain why we're here," Hakim said.

"I'm getting there," Zach said. "That night I also overheard the men talking about this warehouse. I figured that maybe they're storing something here, and we could look for whatever it is."

"Seems like a stretch to me," Hakim said.

"Well," said Kelly patiently, "we *could* look around. The problem is that this place is huge, and we have no idea what they might have hidden here."

At that moment, the front door slammed shut with a loud bang. The room became completely dark.

"Who's there?" Kelly yelled.

"What's going on?" Hakim shouted.

Kelly, Hakim, and Meredith jumped to their feet. Zach rushed with them toward the door. Together, they tried to push it open. But no matter how desperately they tried, the door wouldn't budge.

"Oh, great," Hakim said, feeling his way along the wall. "We're trapped. Springer, you'll pay for this."

The newspaper staff is trapped in an old warehouse, but getting rescued could be even worse.

KELLY'S HOUSE 4

A few hours later, the sound of sirens grew closer and closer. Finally, the crunch of car tires on the gravel outside convinced Kelly and the others that they were finally about to be rescued.

"We're in here!" Kelly screamed at the top of her lungs. She banged on the door as hard as she could. "Let us out!"

"What a relief," Hakim said. "I was starting to worry we might have to spend the rest of our lives here—like the people on *Gilligan's Island*. Zach, we'd have had no choice but to turn to you as a food source."

"Oh, shut up," Zach muttered.

"Hey! We're in here! Open the door! We're in here!" Kelly yelled, ignoring Hakim and Zach. Then the door swung open and light streamed into the windowless warehouse.

"Okay, everybody outside," a uniformed police officer boomed. "Let's go! Keep your hands where we can see them."

"Hey, wait a minute," Meredith said. "We didn't do anything. We were trapped in there!"

Outside, Kelly, Zach, Hakim, and Meredith stood nervously against one of the two police cars while the two cops talked together in low voices. Finally, an angry, bald-headed officer, whose name tag read *Molinari*, turned to them.

"You, you, you, and you," he said, pointing, "get into the squad cars—the back seat."

At the station, Molinari told Kelly and the others to sit down at a long table in a conference room. He glared at them. "I don't want to know what you were doing in that warehouse," he began. "I don't care. I know that if you told me, it would be stupid and it would annoy me, so . . ."

Kelly angrily interrupted. "Excuse me, but do we still have freedom of the press in this country? We're from the *Oak Park Beat*, and we were in that warehouse investigating a story. It was a story about those racist incidents. Of course, you might not feel that great about that. After all, the police . . ."

Hakim elbowed Kelly in the ribs, trying to make her shut up.

"Ow! The police haven't exactly . . ."

Molinari banged his fist on the table, silencing Kelly. "Shut up! You're making me mad. I was going to let you walk out of here. Now you can't go until you reach an adult who is willing to come and pick you up. And if I hear another word out of you before that moment, I'm going to book each one of you for breaking and entering. Got it? Don't talk, just nod."

Everyone nodded.

"You're quick," Molinari said sarcastically. Then he turned to Kelly. "What's your name?"

"Kelly Rivera."

The police officer looked startled. "Rivera? Do you live over on Twenty-third Avenue?"

Kelly nodded.

"Oh, you've got trouble," Molinari said, his tone softening. "You'd better call somebody and get home right now. There's a problem at your house. Nobody's hurt, but . . ." Molinari pushed a telephone from his side of the table across to Kelly.

Shaking, Kelly quickly dialed her mother. As she and her mom talked, the others watched nervously. Seeing their concern, Kelly covered the receiver and turned to her friends. "Somebody sprayed graffiti all over our house. They used red paint, just like they did in the incidents last year!"

After she hung up, Kelly looked around in her purse for the home number of Mr. Andropov, the newspaper adviser. When Molinari called him, he agreed to pick up the *Beat* staff and take them to Kelly's house.

Kelly's head throbbed as she walked through the parking lot to Mr. Andropov's car. Until now, investigating the incidents had seemed like a game or a fascinating TV show. Now everything was frighteningly close to home.

"I have one question," Mr. Andropov said as he

unlocked the door to his beat-up Toyota. "How did the police know you were in the Chambers Warehouse? Who do you think called them?"

Zach and Hakim shook their heads. "I can't imagine," Meredith said. "It's a really good question."

No one spoke again during the five-minute drive. When Mr. Andropov turned onto Kelly's block, they saw police cars parked in her driveway. As they got closer, they could read the graffiti on the white stucco house: "STAY OUT OF PLACES WHERE YOU DON'T BELONG! WATCH OUT!"

Zach is on the trail of the people who vandalized Kelly's house—even if it leads him close to home.

THE LIST 5

"Goodbye, Zachary," Mr. Andropov said as Zach climbed out of his car. "I'll see you at the meeting Tuesday. Meanwhile, don't let this stuff upset you. We'll get to the bottom of it."

"Okay," Zach answered. "Thanks for the ride." Feeling like the world's biggest loser, Zach let himself into his house and wandered into the kitchen.

After things had settled down at Kelly's, Hakim, Kelly, and Meredith went to a hamburger place to figure out what to do next. Although they'd invited Zach to join them, he knew they didn't really want him there. *They think I'm a loser*, he told himself. *Why did I join the newspaper staff, anyway?* He shuffled over to the refrigerator and opened the door.

I've got to do something, Zach thought. *I've got to find out if my dad really knows anything about the incidents. It's not so farfetched. Ever since I can remember, he's hated anybody who wasn't exactly like him. Still, if it turns out he's involved, I don't know what I'll do.*

Realizing he had no appetite, Zach slammed the

refrigerator door shut so hard that he heard jars clang against each other. Then he made a decision. He went to his father's study, flipped on the lights, and started shuffling through piles of papers.

"What am I looking for," Zach said, talking to himself, "a signed confession?" He sorted through the desk and the file cabinets. He found nothing suspicious there. Then he leaned back in his father's chair and surveyed the room.

The small chrome garbage can in the corner gave Zach a glimmer of hope. He remembered an episode of *The X-Files* in which Scully had found key evidence in Mulder's trash. Zach got up, walked over to the can, and looked down into it.

"Oh, gross," he groaned. The trash can was empty except for the remains of a half-eaten apple, some lettuce, and a piece of moldy rye bread.

Zach was getting ready to give up and go to his room to play computer games when an idea suddenly struck him. "Apple!" he cried, looking back down into the garbage. He walked back to his father's desk, yanked open the bottom drawer, and pulled out a laptop computer. Zach knew he was doing something dangerous now. His father would kill him if he found him snooping through his laptop. Still, his dad *had* said· that he wouldn't be home until late that night, so Zach figured that he wouldn't get caught.

He pushed the On button, and the screen came to life. He opened an application and then went to the

pull-down menu that displayed the last three files that had been opened. They all sounded pretty harmless: "plan," "confirmation letter," and "sales forecast memo."

"Plan?" Zach whispered to himself as he opened the file. It appeared on the screen as a list of addresses. It took a minute before Zach realized just why the first address on the list sounded so familiar.

"That's Kelly Rivera's address," he said out loud. "Oh, no." Zach felt lightheaded and dizzy as he scanned the other addresses. Another one, on Jefferson Boulevard, almost jumped off the page at him. He picked up the phone and dialed 411.

"Could I please have the address for Kim's Vegetable Stand?"

As he hung up the phone, tears came to his eyes. The address on the list matched Kim's—a Korean-owned produce market that had been vandalized two weeks before. Sadly, Zach attached the computer to the printer and made a copy of the list. He folded the sheet of paper and stuck it in his back pocket.

He didn't know what to do. Should he go to the burger place and show the list to Kelly and the others? That would mean turning in his own dad. Should he throw out the list, quit the paper, and try to forget everything that had happened?

Just then, Zach heard the study door swing open, and his dad's voice boomed out behind him. "Zachary, get your hands off that machine!"

Zach's dad couldn't possibly be behind the incidents—or could he?

CAUGHT! 6

"You heard me!" Zach's dad yelled as he walked toward his son. "Get away from my computer!" Before his dad could get any closer, Zach shut down the computer and shoved it back into the desk drawer.

"Sorry, Dad," he said, frightened. "It's just that I was trying to . . ."

"Sorry isn't good enough, Zach. Incidents like this make me feel that I just can't trust you."

Zach cowered in his father's desk chair. *How could I have thought it would be okay to ask him about those files on the computer?* Zach thought. *He gets crazy when he's mad. Who knows what he might do?*

"Maybe it's the company you've been keeping," his father continued in a scary voice. "I've said it before, and I'll say it again. People should stick with their own kind. I've seen you spending time with all those people on the newspaper. There's barely a white kid among them."

"Okay, okay," Zach said. He got up and headed for the office door. He couldn't just sit there and listen to his dad's racist nonsense.

"I'm sorry about the computer," he added. "I won't touch it again. I'm going to my room to do my homework now, okay?"

Zach's dad was really frightening him now. He was standing in the doorway between the office and the living room, blocking Zach in the office.

"Dad, can I go to my room now?" Zach pleaded. Then they heard a girl's voice from the living room.

"Hey, Zach! Are you home? The door's wide open!"

Zach and his dad turned away from each other and walked into the living room. When they got to the door, they saw Kelly and Hakim standing in the doorway. Behind them was Officer Molinari, the bald policeman who had caught them at the warehouse.

The police are on the case and looking for evidence—right in Zach's own house.

THE SEARCH 7

Officer Molinari walked through the doorway of Zach's house, moving quickly past Kelly and Hakim. He marched straight up to Zach's dad. Holding out a sheet of paper, he announced, "George Springer, this is a warrant allowing us to search your house."

Zach's mouth dropped open. Minutes before, he'd been so angry that he could have picked up the phone and turned his dad in to the police himself. Now that his father really seemed to be in trouble with the law, he felt awful.

Mr. Springer took a moment to find his voice. "I don't know what this is all about. I'm going to have to call my lawyer. Why are you here? Why are these kids here?"

Zach looked over at Kelly and Hakim. They stood frozen in the doorway, speechless. *Yeah, what are they doing here?* Zach wondered.

"I have no idea why they're here," Molinari answered, glaring at Kelly and Hakim. "They were standing in the doorway when I arrived." He turned to Mr. Springer. "But you've got bigger problems than

those two. We're going to begin searching the entire house. Please clear the area."

Just then, two more police officers walked through the doorway. Zach felt as if he were in a nightmare as he watched the police officers begin searching through drawers and closets.

Mr. Springer rushed to his office to begin making phone calls. Finding himself alone in the middle of the living room, Zach walked over to Kelly and Hakim.

"What *are* you doing here?" he asked them.

For a second, Hakim and Kelly both just stared at him without saying a word. Then Hakim started talking, fast and nervous.

"We thought it would be good to have a newspaper meeting right now. We wanted to decide whether or not to do a story about what happened at Kelly's house—you know, the graffiti and everything. I guess you're, uh, busy. Um, should we leave?"

Kelly interrupted. "Oh, Zach, I'm so sorry about whatever it is that's happening. You must feel terrible. I can't believe your dad is really involved. What should we do?"

"It's okay," Zach muttered, not knowing what else to say.

"I have to tell you something, Zach," Kelly said. "I told Mr. Andropov what you said about your dad. I mentioned that you thought he might know something about the incidents. Mr. Andropov might have told the police. Maybe that's why . . ."

"No, I don't think that could be it," Zach said. "If what they say on TV shows is right, the police have to have some kind of evidence for a judge to give them a warrant. I don't think a third-hand conversation would really count."

"I guess not," Kelly said.

"Do you know what this is about, then, Zach?" Hakim asked.

"No idea," said Zach.

Zach walked out onto the front porch and sat down on the front steps. Kelly and Hakim followed. "Maybe you guys could just hang out for awhile," Zach said.

About thirty minutes later, the police left the house. They walked silently down the steps past Kelly, Hakim, and Zach. They were carrying a few envelopes.

Zach went inside to look for his father. His dad wouldn't speak. He just stared after the cops before taking the stairs upstairs, two at a time.

Zach went back outside. Kelly stood up as she saw the cops getting into their cars.

"I guess I'd better go try to interview them," she said. She smiled apologetically at Zach. "I mean, it could be important for our story, right?"

Kelly ran down the steps and caught up with the police. She stood on the sidewalk and spoke with them for a few minutes.

"They wouldn't even say 'no comment,'" she reported when she came back to the front steps.

She turned to Zach. "I feel so awkward, Zach," Kelly said. "I don't want your dad to go to jail or anything. You don't think that he really did something wrong, do you?"

Zach looked down at his hands, totally confused. What was he supposed to say?

"It doesn't look good, does it?" he managed to say.

"Zach, we're really sorry about this," Hakim said. "But let's not jump to any conclusions. Let's just figure out what we should do next."

While the police search Zach's house, another incident takes place only a block away.

THE CAR 8

Suddenly, as if to save Zach, who felt he might burst into tears at any moment, Meredith came running up the driveway. "I was coming to meet you for the meeting," she said, out of breath. "I was running. Then I saw your Volkswagon, Kelly. It's parked around the corner, right?"

"It's my mom's car," Kelly corrected. "Don't tell me something else is wrong!"

Meredith leaned over and put her hand on Kelly's shoulder. "Kelly, it's the windshield. It's totally smashed. This note was on the driver's seat."

Kelly took the note and read it aloud. "LET THE MYSTERY STAY A MYSTERY, OR YOU'LL REGRET IT. GO BACK TO CHEERLEADING!"

"Well," Kelly huffed. "I guess somebody has a strong opinion about whether we should report this story in the newspaper!"

Zach interrupted Kelly with a loud sigh. "Oh, man," he groaned. "He broke the windshield? Why is this happening to me?"

Meredith looked at Zach as if he'd lost his mind.

"What are you talking about, Zach?" she asked. "You know who did this?"

"Don't be stupid," Zach snapped.

Hakim stood and shook his head impatiently at Zach. "He thinks his dad did it," Hakim explained to Meredith. Then he turned to Zach. "Springer, you're a computer type, right? So be logical! Your dad was inside watching the cops search your house the entire time that the car was parked. There's no way he could have smashed the windshield. He couldn't even have known where the car was parked."

Meredith broke in. "Wait a minute," she said. "You're right, Hakim. Zach's dad couldn't have known the car was there. But who *could* have known the car was there? It was parked on a quiet, dead-end street for a pretty short time. The person who did this had to know where to look."

"That's right," Kelly said. "Meredith, you knew I was coming over here, but that's because I called and told you."

"Right," Meredith said. "I didn't mention it to anyone. Did you tell someone else?"

"I don't remember telling anyone," Kelly said, thinking. "I called you. Hakim was with me . . . ."

"Hey! You did tell someone," Hakim reminded her. "You called your boyfriend, remember?"

"Well, sure, I called Kai," Kelly admitted. "I always tell him what I'm doing. I'm sure he didn't . . ."

"Don't be so sure," Zach said. "You never can tell

about the people closest to you. Believe me, I know what I'm talking about."

"Oh, give me a break," said Kelly.

"Yeah, Zach," Meredith said. "Kai and Kelly have been going out since eighth grade. He's always been sure to keep track of where she is because he tends to worry about things."

"He's the star of the basketball team and one of the most popular kids in school. What does he have to worry about?" Zach muttered.

"Well, for one thing," Meredith said sharply, "his parents died in a car accident when he was only nine years old."

"He's never gotten over it," Kelly said. "They left him alone for a few minutes to pick up some hamburgers, and they never came back. Ever since then, he's just kind of worried a lot."

"That's enough psychology," Hakim said, interrupting. "The point is that strange things definitely seem to be happening to us everywhere we go. What's more, Kai is the only person who's really known everything we've all been doing lately. Maybe you *should* ask him about it, Kelly."

Someone knows every move the newspaper staff is making. Is Kai to blame?

THE FIGHT 9

Kelly sat alone in the last row of the gym bleachers, waiting for basketball practice to end. She didn't really watch the guys play, and she definitely wasn't listening as Coach Mackey gave the team a final pep talk. She was thinking about what she would say to Kai. She caught his eye as he headed toward the locker room. As soon as he saw her, he trotted over.

"Hi!" she said, as he leaned over to kiss her hello.

"This is a surprise," Kai said, smiling. "Did you see that last basket I made? Bronson was defending me, but I faked him out and . . ."

Kelly shook her head before he went any further. "I didn't come to talk about basketball," she said. "This is something really serious."

His smile vanished. "What's up?" he asked.

Kelly didn't waste any time. She started telling him about everything that had happened that day—including the conversation she'd just had with the others. "Once we started talking about it," Kelly said, "we realized that you're the only one who's always known exactly what we were planning."

Kai's face clouded over with anger. "What are you saying, Kelly?" he snapped. "You think I'm involved? I mean, don't you know me a little better than that?"

"Of course, I know you're not involved." Kelly said. "Still, you have to admit that I barely even cross the street without calling you and letting you know my precise plans."

"So what are you getting at?" Kai asked, still angry.

"I told you that you should keep all the newspaper stuff a secret," Kelly said. "Have you told anybody at all about what we've been doing?"

"Oh, gosh, yes!" Kai said sarcastically. "It almost slipped my mind, but I have been walking up to evil-looking people on the street and playing tape recordings of our conversations. I'm sorry. I didn't think you'd mind!"

"Kai," Kelly tried to interrupt.

"I think you're losing your mind," Kai continued. "You've got all these little secrets. You're doing all this investigating. What makes you think that you're so important that somebody would be going after you and your little newspaper pals?"

Kelly was horrified. In the four years that she and Kai had been going out, he had never talked to her this way.

"Well," she said, raising her voice, "now that you've told me how you really feel, could you please answer my question?"

Just then, Martin Beckwith, the team's center,

walked out of the locker room. When he saw Kelly and Kai on the bleachers, he headed toward them.

"Oh, great," Kelly muttered under her breath.

"Hey, Kai," he said. "Buenos dias, Kelly. I'm surprised to see you here, senorita. Kai told me you'd given up watching basketball. He said that you've decided to devote every last minute to the pursuit of truth, justice, and the news. I hear that a lot of really interesting things have been going on."

Kelly's whole face hardened as she gave Kai a look. "Oh, what have you heard about?" she asked, turning to Martin and trying to sound casual.

"Oh, I heard about that guy playing dead at the old Chambers warehouse. Let's see, what else? You guys nearly got arrested. That was pretty funny. Oh, then, some creep painted graffiti on your house."

Kelly couldn't believe her ears. "Kai, you *have* been talking to people," she yelled. "How could I ever have trusted you? I must have been out of my mind!"

Kelly stormed home and called Meredith. "He's been telling everything—and I mean everything—to that idiot Martin Beckwith," Kelly said. "I can't believe it—Martin Beckwith! He's always making jokes about me being Mexican American and talking to me in his lame Spanish."

"Why would Kai tell our secrets?" Meredith asked. "It doesn't seem like him. Do you think he's feeling left out because you're editor of the newspaper?"

"I guess," Kelly answered. "He'd been thinking all summer about how I was going to be a cheerleader, cheering him on to victory and all that."

"Instead you've been so busy with the paper that you haven't even made it to any practices," Meredith said. "You used to go all the time. He must be disappointed. Maybe he's even mad."

"He must be," said Kelly. "I never realized he was like that."

"Are you going to call him?" Meredith asked.

"Are you kidding me?" Kelly fumed angrily. "After what he did, I'm never speaking to him again." She paused for a second before going on. "I guess one good thing has come from this, though. We now have a suspect."

"Martin?" Meredith asked.

"Martin," Kelly repeated. "Definitely."

Kelly's romance is definitely over, but Meredith's may just be beginning.

THE ROMANCE 10

A few days later, Kelly was at her wits' end. The newspaper staff seemed no closer to solving the mystery of the incidents. Sure, there were bits and pieces of evidence. But their information wasn't solid enough to justify writing a story.

"I'm losing hope," Kelly told Meredith and Zach as she sipped a chocolate shake at their favorite hamburger place.

"Well, at least we've got a good newspaper going," Zach said. "Maybe we haven't gotten the *big* story, but everything else is going great!"

"Zach! How unlike you," Meredith teased. "You're actually looking on the bright side!"

Kelly laughed, then stood up. "I've got to do some regular old homework," she said. "If I don't get my grades up, this year is really going to be a disaster."

Alone at the table, Meredith and Zach chatted for a while. Then Meredith reached for her backpack. "I guess I'd better get going," she said.

"Uh, wait," Zach said nervously. "Do you have to go right now?"

"No, not this minute," Meredith answered.

"Meredith," Zach began, "there's something I've been wanting to ask you. If you have to go, though, it's no problem. I'll tell, uh, ask, you some other time. It's no big deal really."

Meredith, catching Zach's nervousness, put her pack back down on the seat and waited. "What is it?"

"I was just wondering if maybe we could go somewhere—uh, together, I mean." Zach's face was even redder than his hair. "I mean, just the two of us on Friday?"

A huge smile crept over Meredith's face. "Sure," she answered. "That would be great."

Later, sitting on the edge of her parents' bed, Meredith talked to Kelly on the only phone in the house that allowed any privacy. "I guess Zach is a social reject, but so am I," she said. "Anyway, we get along."

"You're not a reject, and neither is he," Kelly said. "I've really gotten to like him. He's smart and nice. You'll make a great couple." A sad note crept into her voice. "Now I guess I'll find out how you felt all these years while I had a boyfriend and you didn't."

"Don't worry, Kel. I'm not going to start ignoring you or anything. Besides, we're not a couple. We're just going to the movies together." She sighed. "I can't believe I'm sixteen and just now having my first date."

Friday night, Meredith and Zach were in line at the movie theater. The same thought was going through both of their minds. After all this time being jealous of happy couples waiting in line at the movies, it was great to be one of those couples. Zach smiled at Meredith. Then his gaze wandered across the street, to a twenty-four-hour copy shop. "That place is always busy," he remarked.

"It sure is," Meredith agreed. "I wonder why people need so many copies."

Uh-oh, Zach thought. *This is a really stupid conversation. Why can't I ever think of anything interesting to say?*

Then Meredith interrupted his thoughts. "Look, there's that idiot Martin Beckwith," she said. "See him? He's walking into the copy shop right now."

Zach squinted. "Oh, yeah," he said as the basketball player came into focus. "And check it out. I think I know that big guy with him!"

"Who is it?" Meredith asked.

"I'm pretty sure he's some real estate buddy of my dad," Zach said, excited. "What's he doing with Beckwith? It seems suspicious, doesn't it, to see those two together like that?"

"Should we follow them?"

"We'll lose our place in line."

"So what!"

Zach and Meredith secretly shadow two suspects—
and find out more than they would have guessed.

The Copy Shop

Zach and Meredith stood in the alley next to the copy shop. "I guess we shouldn't go in," Meredith said.

"Right," Zach agreed. "The whole idea of following someone is to stay out of sight."

"Still, Zach, you know . . ." Meredith began, then trailed off.

"What?" Zach prodded.

"I hate to say this, but Martin Beckwith probably doesn't even know who we are," Meredith said.

"I know what you mean," Zach said. "He's one of those guys who only notices the animals at the top of the food chain."

"So let's go in," said Meredith. "We can buy some envelopes or something."

As the two of them went in, they saw that the copy shop was packed with people. "There they are," Zach whispered to Meredith, as he wandered over to an envelope display. "They're standing by the counter."

"So does that guy with Martin still look familiar?" Meredith whispered.

"Yeah, I've definitely seen him with my dad.

They've done a couple of real estate deals together."

"Look!" Meredith whispered, still staring. "He's giving Beckwith money!"

It was like a scene from a movie. The older man pulled a bulging wallet out of his back pocket, opened it, and started putting bills into Beckwith's open hand.

"Wow," Zach said. "That's really suspicious!"

The man put his wallet back in his pocket, nodded at Beckwith, then headed out the door.

Meredith and Zach were in a frenzy. "What should we do?" Meredith hissed. "Should we split up?"

"No!" Zach whispered back. "You could get killed!"

"Oh, spare me," Meredith said.

"I'm not kidding!" Zach said.

"You could get killed too," Meredith said. "Being a guy doesn't make you immortal."

Then she glanced out the window. "The real estate guy is gone, anyway! He just drove away in a red sportscar."

"He got away," Zach said. "It's my fault."

"Oh, it doesn't matter," Meredith said.

"We can stay with Beckwith," Zach replied.

"It looks like he's waiting for copies. No, wait! He's going to the back!"

Beckwith walked to the back of the store and into the men's room. A minute later, a new clerk walked up to the counter.

"This is our chance," Zach said. "Come on. Let's go see if we can find out what Beckwith is copying."

Zach walked to the counter. "Uh, my name is Beckwith," he said to the clerk. "I'm getting some copies made of . . . something, and I just realized that I might have forgotten to correct a mistake. Could I take a look at it?"

"Sure," the clerk replied, turning around to retrieve the document.

Meredith nervously watched the door to the men's room. Finally, the clerk returned.

"Here you go," said the clerk, handing Zach a sheet of paper.

"Don't read it now," Meredith whispered to Zach. "Go to the machine and make a copy. Then let's get out of here."

Zach quickly ran off a copy. Then he returned the original to the clerk, who looked at him strangely.

"Let's get out of here," Zach said, pulling Meredith toward the door.

Once outside, Meredith and Zach ran down the street. They paused to catch their breath. "I can't believe we just did that," Meredith said.

"Ready to hear it?" Zach asked.

"Definitely," Meredith said.

"It's a letter," said Zach. "'To all concerned citizens of Oak Park: I am a former member of the maintenance staff of the now-abandoned Chambers Warehouse . . .'"

"The Chambers Warehouse again!" Meredith said.

Zach continued reading, "'It has come to my

44

attention that our city politicians are planning to build low-income housing on the site. Before this plan becomes a reality, I must inform all of you that the warehouse and the land surrounding it are poisoned with mercury and other toxic chemicals. The area is not fit for human habitation!'"

"This is bizarre," Meredith said. "I doubt that the real estate guy ever worked in that warehouse."

"Even if he did," Zach added, "why would he be writing this letter? And why would Martin Beckwith be involved?"

Why are people all over Oak Park receiving copies of that mysterious letter?

THE LETTER 12

A few days later, Kelly trudged up the stairs of her house. It was 4:30, and she was exhausted. She congratulated herself on avoiding all after-school activities that day. *I'm going to sit in front of the television and stare at MTV until dinner*, she promised herself. *Then I'm going to go to my room to read fashion magazines.* It had been a tough few weeks, and she was getting more and more frustrated and depressed.

Before going inside, she checked the mailbox. "Nothing for me, of course," she said aloud as she shuffled through the pile of bills, advertisements, and catalogs. She had been secretly hoping that Kai would write her a romantic letter, begging her to come back to him. It hadn't happened. She wished she could put the idea out of her mind. That way she wouldn't have to experience that awful feeling in her stomach every time she picked up the mail and there was nothing there for her.

Sighing, she went inside. She plopped down on the couch and turned on MTV. An hour later, her mother arrived home from work.

"Kelly," she said, "you should see this strange letter we got. It's about the Chambers Warehouse."

"You're kidding," Kelly said, lifting herself from the couch. "Does it mention toxic waste?"

"It does, as a matter of fact," her mom said. "How did you know?"

"Let me see it."

Kelly examined the letter. As she'd suspected, it was the same one Zach and Meredith had made a copy of the weekend before. Then she looked at the envelope. The label was computer printed. It had probably been mailed to lots of people.

The phone rang, and Kelly's mom answered. It was their next-door neighbor, Mrs. Washington.

"Ask her if she got the letter," Kelly whispered, waving the envelope in her mother's face.

"Gloria, did you get a letter about the Chambers Warehouse?" Kelly's mother covered the mouthpiece of the receiver and whispered to Kelly. "She did. That's why she called. She's worried."

The next day, Kelly met with the newspaper staff. "It seems that lots of people in Oak Park got a copy of that letter yesterday," Kelly told the group. "Understandably, people are worried about being poisoned by the toxic waste, especially people who might be eligible for housing at the warehouse site. We may be the only ones in town who have any idea who sent the letter out."

"I guess that means we have a scoop," Meredith

said. "We'll run a story in the next issue of the *Oak Park Beat.*"

"We could," Kelly said. "Luckily, we have six days before that issue comes out. By then, we should be able to find out more about what the letter really means."

"That would help," Hakim said. "I hate to say it, but right now we don't have much of a scoop. What could we say?" Hakim lowered his voice to imitate the local news anchor. "Ladies and gentlemen, the letter seems to have been mailed by a real-estate agent who's a friend of Zach's father—but we don't know his name. Martin Beckwith, a stupid basketball player who's kind of a racist, helped him carry out the evil deed."

Kelly interrupted. "You're right. We have a lot of unanswered questions. First of all, is there still a plan to build housing on the site of the Chambers Warehouse? I haven't heard anything about it recently. Second, is there really a toxic waste problem there? Then there's the *big* question: What does all this have to do with the incidents?"

Toxic waste has something to do with the incidents.
Finding out what could be dangerous.

THE PROTESTS 13

The next day, Kelly got on the phone. After a few calls, she turned to her mother. "Okay," she said, "we have a plan. I'm meeting my friends from the paper down at the city planner's office. We'll find out once and for all if the letter's telling the truth."

Kelly's mother smiled nervously. "Just make sure you drive carefully, Kelly," she said. "It's raining and the roads are slick."

Kelly nodded. She had a feeling that her mom was worried about more than the roads.

Kelly got into her mother's old Volkswagon. As she backed out of the driveway, she noticed a dark blue station wagon stopped at the corner behind her. As she started down the street, the other car started moving in the same direction. *Just a coincidence*, Kelly told herself. *It's nothing to worry about.*

Still, as Kelly drove toward the city planner's office, the station wagon took every turn she did. The car was just a little too far away for her to see the driver clearly. *This is getting scary*, Kelly thought. *I'd better lose this guy.* She soon had her chance. At the next stoplight, she sped through the yellow light. The blue station wagon had to stop.

When Kelly finally pulled into the parking lot at the planner's office, she had another surprise. Although it was drizzling, about a hundred people stood outside protesting. They carried signs that said "Stop Toxic Waste Now!" and "Don't Build Our Houses on Poison!"

Pushing her way inside, Kelly found Hakim, Meredith, and Zach. "Someone tried to follow me here," she said.

"Did you lose them?" Hakim asked.

"I think so."

"Good. We'll talk about it later. Right now, we have to go to Ms. Chopra's office. She's waiting for us."

Ms. Chopra, the city planner, greeted Kelly and the others at her office door. After they all sat down, Kelly was the first to speak. "Is it true that the Chambers Warehouse is set to become a low-income housing site?"

"Yes, it's true," said the small, dark-haired woman.

"Is it also true that the site is contaminated with toxic waste?" Hakim loaded his film as he spoke.

"Absolutely not. The state Environmental Protection Agency has given it a clean bill of health."

"It may be hard to convince all those people outside that it's safe," Hakim said as he snapped a picture.

Ms. Chopra sighed. "You're right. So we may not be able to use the site. If that turns out to be the case,

the reasons would be political, not environmental."

"You mean that people's protests could create a problem?" Zach asked.

Ms. Chopra nodded. "If this keeps up, we'll have to find another site farther out of town."

"What would happen to Chambers Warehouse then?" Meredith asked.

"The city would probably sell it to the highest bidder," Ms. Chopra answered.

After the interview, Kelly and her friends went back outside. The protesters still stood in the light rain. Kelly put up her big umbrella, and the others crowded around her.

"This is too strange," Hakim said. "How did all these people even know to protest here?"

"They got the letter," said Zach. "And I think that I might have found the mailing list on my dad's computer. He had the addresses of everyone eligible for low-income housing."

"Interesting," said Meredith. "So maybe your dad was involved in the incidents after all."

"It's still not clear what all this has to do with the incidents," said Hakim. "Besides, that really wasn't even my point."

"What was your point?" asked Zach.

"It just seems odd," Hakim responded. "How did these people know to come to this particular place? I had to make ten or twelve calls just to find out that the person we needed to talk to was the city planner."

Meredith nodded. "You're right." She looked over at Kelly who was silently staring off into space. "What do you think, Kel?"

Kelly shook her head. "I think I didn't lose the blue station wagon that was following me after all. Look. It's parked right over there."

Everyone turned in the direction she was pointing. "There's somebody still in it," said Zach.

"There is," said Kelly, "and I'm going to find out who it is right now."

Kelly started walking through the rain toward the mysterious blue car.

A strange car has been following Kelly. Has an old friend become a new enemy?

Mystery Man 14

Meredith watched Kelly stride off across the parking lot. Then she turned to the others. "Come on, guys. We can't let her talk to that guy by herself. Let's go." The three started off and caught up with Kelly just as she reached the station wagon.

At that moment, the driver got out, slamming the door behind him. "Hi, Kel," he said. Kelly's heart nearly stopped. It was Kai.

"Kai! Just what do you think you're doing?" Kelly put her hand on the side of the station wagon to steady herself. "You scared me to death. You tailed me here— and in a strange car."

Kai looked surprised. "Oh, I'm sorry. Grandpa bought this car last week. He said I could borrow it because I really needed to talk to you. I drove over to your house, but you were just leaving. So I followed you over here."

"Uh-oh," said Hakim, turning to Zach and Meredith. "He *had* to talk to her. This looks seriously romantic. Maybe we should disappear."

"No," said Kai. "It's not romance."

It wasn't romance? Kelly felt as if she'd been slugged in the stomach. Those were definitely not the words she wanted to hear. "Of course it's not romance, Hakim," she said.

She turned to Kai, "So just why *were* you looking for me?" she asked. She made her voice cold and business-like.

"Politics," said Kai, swallowing hard. "Ever since you got suspicious of Martin, I've been watching him. Now it turns out that he's the one organizing these protests about toxic waste. He's handing out leaflets to get low-income people to come demonstrate. He's got everyone convinced that he's concerned about their health, but . . ."

"He's not," said Kelly. "But that's not surprising."

"There's more," said Kai. "Martin's working with this real-estate developer. They've got everyone angry about toxic waste. If the protests keep up, the city will drop the low-income housing plan. Then they'll have to sell the warehouse to the highest bidder."

"Right," said Meredith. "Of course, the lies about toxic waste mean that the highest bid will be low. The guy will get the warehouse practically for nothing. That's pretty evil, huh?"

"On the plus side," said Hakim, "this is a big story. It's news we can break."

"The problem is that we still don't know who this real estate guy is," said Meredith, "or what this all has to do with the incidents."

"Would your dad know?" Kai asked Zach. "He's involved in real estate. I remember you thought he might know something about all this."

"I'm just not sure," Zach said.

"I think we should go talk to Zach's dad now." Kai was taking charge of the group just as he took charge of the basketball team.

Kelly couldn't stand it any longer. Not only was Kai no longer interested in her, he was pushing his way into her story. "Oh, look at Mr. Detective," she said. "You gave me so much grief about this story. Now that we're about to solve the mystery, you want to waltz in and take the credit."

"That's not it," Kai began.

"I'm not stupid," said Kelly. "I definitely understand what's going on."

Kai's face crumpled. "If that's the way you feel," he said, "I'm getting out of here." He stormed back to the station wagon without another word. The door slammed behind him. Within seconds, he was gone.

Kelly just stood there. *I will not cry*, she told herself. *I will not cry.*

"Kelly, why did you go and do that?" demanded Meredith.

"I don't know," said Kelly. "I just didn't want him pushing into everything." She didn't want to tell Meredith the truth in front of Zach and Hakim.

"Well, Kai was right about one thing," said Zach.

"He was right about a lot of things," Meredith said.

"But what are you talking about in particular, Zach?"

"We should talk to my dad."

"Are you sure?" Meredith asked.

"It's time," Zach said.

"All right," said Hakim. "Let's go."

Meredith, Hakim, and Zach started toward Zach's car. Kelly made no move to go with them.

"Kelly, are you going to follow us in your car?" Meredith asked her.

"Go on without me," Kelly said. "I've got a few things to do first."

Kai thinks solving the mystery is the key to Kelly's heart. But will his investigation get him locked up?

Danger!
15

"What was bothering Kelly?" Hakim asked Meredith as they drove off in Zach's car. "She seemed really weird. She wasn't acting like herself at all."

"That's right," said Zach. "She didn't even care about talking to my dad."

"She must be upset about Kai," Meredith said. "She'd been hoping that they'd get back together. He didn't seem that interested."

"Are you crazy? No guy would come chasing over to City Hall like that if he wasn't completely in love," Hakim said.

"That's for sure," Zach agreed. "Then, the way she acted made me think she couldn't stand him."

Meredith sighed. "So maybe it's just a misunderstanding. Anyway, we're here at your house now. Let's see if we can find your father."

"I don't think he's here," Zach said, looking around. "His car isn't in the driveway."

"Do you have any idea where he might have gone?" Hakim asked.

"Not really. Today is his day off."

"So we're stuck. Why didn't you think about this before?" Hakim said impatiently.

"Let's think of another plan," said Meredith. "Is there any other way we can find out about this real estate guy? Zach's dad couldn't be the only one in town who'd know something about him."

Meanwhile, back in town, Kai drove down one street after another. He didn't understand why Kelly was so angry. He'd thought that she'd be happy to have the information about Martin Beckwith—maybe happy enough to take him back. Instead, she'd yelled at him. Well, Kai thought, he had one more chance to get her attention. He'd find Martin. Then he'd question him and get to the bottom of this whole mess.

When he finally spotted Martin handing out fliers on Front Street, Kai parked the car. Then he practically sprinted over to him. "Hey, Martin," he said. "We need to talk."

"Maybe later," Martin said. He went right on handing out leaflets.

"Not later—now," Kai said, grabbing Martin's arm. "I know everything that you've been doing. I know about the incidents." It was just a guess, but Kai planned to act like he knew what he was talking about.

"Ah, man, you are so wrong." Martin kept grumbling, but he followed Kai around the corner to a deserted alley. Absolutely no one was around, and only one car, a gray minivan with tinted windows, was parked there. Since the alley was so private, Kai thought, maybe Martin would finally want to open up and talk. It was such an empty stretch of pavement that a bomb could go off and no one would hear it.

"So what is it that you think you know, anyway?" Martin asked. He didn't look Kai in the face.

"I know why the real estate guy wants you to scare everybody about toxic waste," Kai said. "He's trying to stop that housing project and get Chambers Warehouse for nothing. Plus, I know that you're the one responsible for the incidents. It's my guess, though, that they weren't your idea. You're just working for him."

"You don't really know anything. You're just acting like you do," Martin said.

"Wrong. Why not just tell me the truth? The cops will be here any minute. I asked them to meet me here." Kai didn't know if his lie would work, but it was worth a try.

"Oh, man," Martin groaned. "I hope they understand. It wasn't my idea. It was Dempsey's. I never meant to get that involved in this mess . . ."

Kai interrupted. "Dempsey is the real estate guy? The friend of Zach's dad?"

"Right," Martin said. "He was paying me just to scare people a little. I never really hurt anyone."

"All the same, you did a lot of harm. What made you do it?"

Martin sighed. "Dad's really sick. He's been out of

61

work. We needed the money to pay all our bills."

Well, that was a reason, Kai thought. He sort of understood why Martin had done what he'd done—but there could be no really good excuse. "What was Dempsey's motive?"

"Why don't you ask me?" Kai's head swiveled toward the unfamiliar voice. A hulking blond man, heavy but well muscled, stood next to the black minivan, about ten feet away.

Kai swallowed hard. "You must be Mr. Dempsey."

Dempsey didn't answer. He just pulled a rope out of the back of the van as Kai watched, wondering what the guy planned to do with it. Dempsey walked toward him and Martin, then grabbed Kai by the arm.

"Help me tie him up," he barked to Martin.

"What good is that going to do?" Martin definitely sounded uncomfortable.

"You want to get paid, don't you, Martin?" Dempsey asked. "Or do you want the bank to take away your dad's house?"

Martin hesitated for a second. Then he helped Dempsey with the rope. They tied Kai's hands behind his back, then roped his feet together. Kai struggled, but he couldn't break away. He didn't even bother to scream. It was pointless since no one would be able to hear him.

Once they'd tied him up, Dempsey and Martin pushed Kai into the back seat of the van. "What are we going to do with him?" Martin asked.

"He knows too much," Dempsey said. "We have to get rid of him."

"Get rid of him?" Martin's voice shook. "How?"

"I don't know yet. I have to think about it. Meanwhile, we'll stash him in the warehouse."

Martin walked to the back of the van to close the door. "Chambers Warehouse?" he asked. Now, Kai thought, Martin's voice seemed abnormally loud.

"Yeah. Get moving," Dempsey grunted. Then he and Martin climbed into the van's front seat, and Dempsey turned the key in the ignition.

Kai knows who's responsible for the incidents. But will he live to tell the story?

THE TRUTH 16

Martin and Mr. Dempsey dragged Kai out of the van and in through the front door of the warehouse. Kai couldn't believe what a mess he'd gotten himself into, and so far he hadn't thought of any way to get out of it. The one idea that he did have was that the longer he stalled, the better off he'd be. "Could I at least know why?" he asked. "What was your motive for the incidents?"

Dempsey laughed. "You wouldn't understand. You're not a real American. The fact was that somebody had to make this town safe for real Americans. You and your friends don't belong here. I wanted to scare all of you away." He shoved Kai down on a sack in the dark, dusty warehouse.

"You're talking about hate," Kai said, struggling, but failing, to rise to his feet. "Hatred for anyone different from you."

"No, you've got it wrong. We had a nice, quiet town here, just the way we liked it. Then some people wanted to let a bunch of immigrants and other undesirable people live here. There's no way I could let that happen, not in Oak Park, pal. So when the so-called 'incidents' didn't scare them away, Einstein junior here helped me spread the rumor about the toxic waste. I figured the best way to keep the outsiders out was to make them think someone was trying to trick them into moving in."

Kai said, "Your whole scheme is about hate. You're just so full of hate that you can't recognize it anymore."

Dempsey just laughed as he pulled a new lock out of his pocket. He and Martin began walking toward the door.

"I have one more question," Kai said, "before you leave me here—to die or whatever. Was Zach Springer's dad involved?"

"You are the curious one," Dempsey said, chuckling. "No, he wasn't part of it. I thought he was on my side. But once I sent him my list of undesirable people, he bolted. You can bet I didn't trust him with any of my plans. But that's enough of your questions now. The only thing I'm wondering now is whether to leave you here to starve—or to come back later and finish the job more personally."

Then, suddenly and without warning, Dempsey gave Martin a push that sent him stumbling toward Kai. "You know too much, too," Dempsey said. Then he stepped out, slamming the warehouse door. The two boys heard the lock snap into place behind him.

Kai peered over at Martin, who sprawled a few feet away from him. "Unless we think of something soon, it looks like we're both in serious trouble now."

Martin looked dazed. "I doubt it," he said finally. "Someone will rescue us."

Kai stared at Martin with surprise. He was about to say something more when tires squealed in the driveway. "Let's try to make a plan," Kai said. "It sounds like he's left."

"No, it sounds more like someone else is coming to the warehouse," said Martin. "Maybe it's the cops."

"Why would the cops be here?" Kai asked.

Even before Martin could answer, the warehouse door swung open and Officer Molinari stood in the doorway blinking into the dark.

"Beckwith? Wong? Are you in there?"

"We're here," said Martin, "but Kai's tied up. Can you help me get him loose?"

When Kai and Martin walked out of the warehouse and into the bright sunlight outside, Kai saw that Dempsey stood next to a second police officer, his hands cuffed behind him.

"You'll be glad to know that this man's under arrest," said Officer Molinari. "Of course, we're going to need you fellows as witnesses."

"How did you know to come here?" asked Kai. "I thought we'd probably die in there."

Officer Molinari nodded toward the parking lot. "Your friend, Ms. Rivera, alerted us."

Kelly? Kai looked around in confusion. Yes, there was Kelly, almost in tears, but still smiling.

She ran into his arms. "Kai, you're safe!" she said. "I was so worried!"

"What happened? How did you . . . ?"

"I followed you from the planner's office. I wanted to say I was sorry. Then I saw Mr. Dempsey throw you into that van. Luckily, Martin saw me. He said where they were taking you, really loud. So all I had to do was find the police and tell them."

"You saved our lives," Kai said.

"You solved the mystery."

Kai and Kelly kissed. They looked up only when they heard laughter behind them.

"See," Zach told Meredith and Hakim. "I told you he was crazy about her."

"Well," Meredith retorted, "I told both of you that she liked him too."

Kai and Kelly pulled apart in embarrassment. "Where did you come from?" Kai asked. "Weren't you going to see Zach's dad?"

"He wasn't home," answered Hakim. "Then we realized that Martin was the man most likely to have the information we needed. So we started looking for him. We found Kelly, and the police . . . and a lot more than we bargained for."

"You kids were thinking like real detectives," said Officer Molinari. "You'll really get a chance to see the justice system in action once we get this guy to trial."

He turned to Martin. "I'm afraid you'll have to come down to the station with me. We'll have to charge you as an accessory. However, the fact that you helped save Kai's life will be a factor in your favor."

Hakim snapped a few pictures as Officer Molinari led Dempsey away, with Martin following sheepishly behind. "For once, we've got a big story to break," he told the others.

"Big?" Kelly asked. "It's *huge*. I'm putting it on the front page with a headline three inches high."

"This is so great," said Meredith. "Now that we've solved the mystery, maybe Ms. Bauer will even bring back the cheerleading squad."

"Cheerleading?" Kelly said. "She might, I guess. I'd almost forgotten that she'd said that."

"You don't sound excited at all," said Kai.

"It's hard to get excited about cheerleading," said Kelly, "once you've got news in your blood."

DID YOU LIKE THIS BOOK?

Here are two other READ 180 Paperbacks that you might like to read.

ZERO TOLERANCE

A high school takes matters into its own hands and suspends forty-eight students! Is this drastic solution really fair?

BY ADAM GRANT

THE ADVENTURES OF CAPTAIN UNDERPANTS

The story of the wackiest superhero of all time: Captain Underpants!

BY DAV PILKEY